To all the grandmothers who don't need capes or superpowers to be our heroes.

First Edition

Copyright @2021 Suzette Perez-Tate and Anisa Delaluz
All rights reserved.

ISBN: 978-0-578-92366-6

No part of this book may be reproduced or transmitted in any form or by any means, electronic or mechanical, including photocopying, recording, or by any information storage and retrieval system - except by a reviewer who may quote brief quotations in a review to be printed in a magazine, newspaper or on the Web - without permission in writing from the publisher. Illustrations by Hayley Moore.

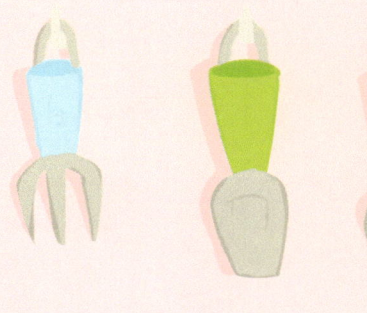

The Grands

Modern-Day  Grandparent

Time With My Grand

written by Suzette Perez-Tate
and Anisa Delaluz

illustrated by Hayley Moore

Spending time with your **grandmother** can be quite a joy.

Grandmothers are caring and have lots to teach. The Grands enjoy spending time with their grandchildren.

Here's how Charlotte spends time with her Nana.

When Nana can't visit, she makes sure to call me whenever she can.

Nana is a manager and gets to work at home in her office.

I like to write letters to Nana. She loves receiving them.

Sometimes, Nana surprises me by sending a package of our favorite snack, **popcorn!**

I appreciate Nana finding ways to spend time with me.

Where does your grandmother live?

Sofia's Glamma lives close by to her.
Here's how they spend time together.

My Glamma picks me up each day after school.
We go to the park when the day is nice.

Glamma helps me with my homework, and I help her with her online boutique.

We make a great team!

When Mommy and Daddy work late, I eat dinner with Glamma.
Sometimes we bake chocolate chip cookies!

I enjoy spending time with Glamma when Mommy and Daddy are at work.

Does your grandmother watch after you when your parents are at work?

Grandma Lee doesn't watch Jordan after school, but she visits often.
Here's how Jordan spends time with his Grandma Lee.

My Grandma Lee is a student like me.
She is in college, and I'm in grade school.

Grandma Lee wants to be an art professor. She taught me how to draw a dinosaur, an airplane, and a cartoon character.

We like to do many activities together. My favorite thing to do is looking through the telescope.

When my Grandpa Lee was alive, he used to show me the planets in the night sky.

Now Grandma Lee shows me.

Grandma Lee is never too busy to do activities with me.

What activities does your grandmother do with you?

Lola Bella and Izzy practice softball together. Here's how Izzy spends time with her Lola Bella.

My Lolo and Lola Bella don't live in the same house, but I get to spend time with both of them at my softball games.

We don't always win. Lola Bella says it is more important to have fun.

My Lola Bella works as a flight attendant.
Whenever she goes to a new city,
she brings me back a magnet.

One day, I would like to be a pilot, so I can see the cities that stick on my refrigerator.

What gifts do you receive from your grandmother?

Mimi likes to surprise Alex with science kits.
Here's how Alex and Mimi spend time together.

My Mimi and I spend time together doing science experiments. The other day we made a homemade compass.

Mimi is a Doctor.

When I get sick, Mom and Dad call Mimi to come and check on me. I'm Mimi's most important patient. Mimi makes sure I wash my hands often, eat vegetables, and get exercise.

I learned that riding a bike makes your bones stronger. It also helps your joints, like your knees and ankles.

Mimi teaches me good habits because she cares for me a lot.

What good habits does your grandmother teach you?

G-Ram taught Jake how to care for a garden.
Here's how Jake spends time with his G-Ram.

My G-Ram owns a restaurant, and Grandpa Jo is the chef.
I spend time with G-Ram in the garden behind the restaurant.

Things are different living with G-Ram than with Mommy, but not in a bad way. I get to play with Aunt Sandra, and it's lots of fun!

On the weekends, we go to G-Ram's restaurant and eat dinner together. I get to order anything I want from the menu.

One day, Mommy will be back. For now, I'm ok living with my G-Ram. I know she loves me.

How does your grandmother show you she loves you?

As you can see, there are many ways to spend time with your grand.

Now I want to know how do you spend time with your Grand?

MY GRAND AND I ......

Made in the USA
Columbia, SC
18 February 2025